This book belongs to . . . .

Ice Sausages

Fairy Cakes

Star Pie

Knickerbocker Glory

Wibbly Wobbly Jelly

Fairydust Flan

Banana Pizza

Splodgy Pudding

Funday Sundae

Jumping Jelly Beans

For Agnes

with thanks to Penny and Jiffany

EGMONT
We bring stories to life

First published in Great Britain 2008
by Egmont UK Limited
239 Kensington High Street
London W8 6SA

Text and Illustrations copyright © Sue Heap 2008

The moral rights of the author and illustrator have been asserted

ISBN 978 14052 3643 0 (Hardback)
ISBN 978 14052 3644 7 (Paperback)

1 3 5 7 9 10 8 6 4 2

A CIP catalogue record for this title is available from the British Library

Printed in China

The FABULOUS FAIRY FEAST

by Sue Heap

EGMONT

One day in Fairyland, Lizzie Little-Fairy was riding her special pink bicycle and reading her favourite book when her pet frog, Burp, appeared with an invitation from the Fairy Queen.

The invitation read like this:

Dear Lizzie Little-Fairy
You are royally invited
to a fabulous midnight
feast tonight at the
magical meeting place.
Please bring your
best pet.

The Fairy
Queen

Lizzie
Little-Fairy
Land

So Lizzie Little-Fairy put Burp in the basket of her special pink bicycle and off they went.

over a cloud

They cycled up into the sky,

The Woods

and down,

down,

down,

into . . .

Which is where they saw
all their friends!

Ellie and her elephant,
Kirsty and her cat,
Fiona and her fox,
Bertie and his bat.
Gloria brought her goose,
Henry brought a hen,
Betsy had her bear,
A rabbit was with Ben.
And Mark brought his shark
(who didn't like the woods
and didn't like the dark!)

And everyone loved
Lizzie's pink bicycle. They all wished
they could have a go on it!

At the arrival of the Queen,
all the fairies curtseyed and all the pets bowed.
"Welcome fairies and your pets," she said,
"to my fabulous midnight feast!"

Everyone clapped and cheered.
In all the excitement, Burp
hopped off Lizzie's head . . .

. . . and landed in the
Queen's bag, which
was being carried
by Maurice the Monkey . . .

. . . who thought it would
be funny to take it up into
the tallest tree!

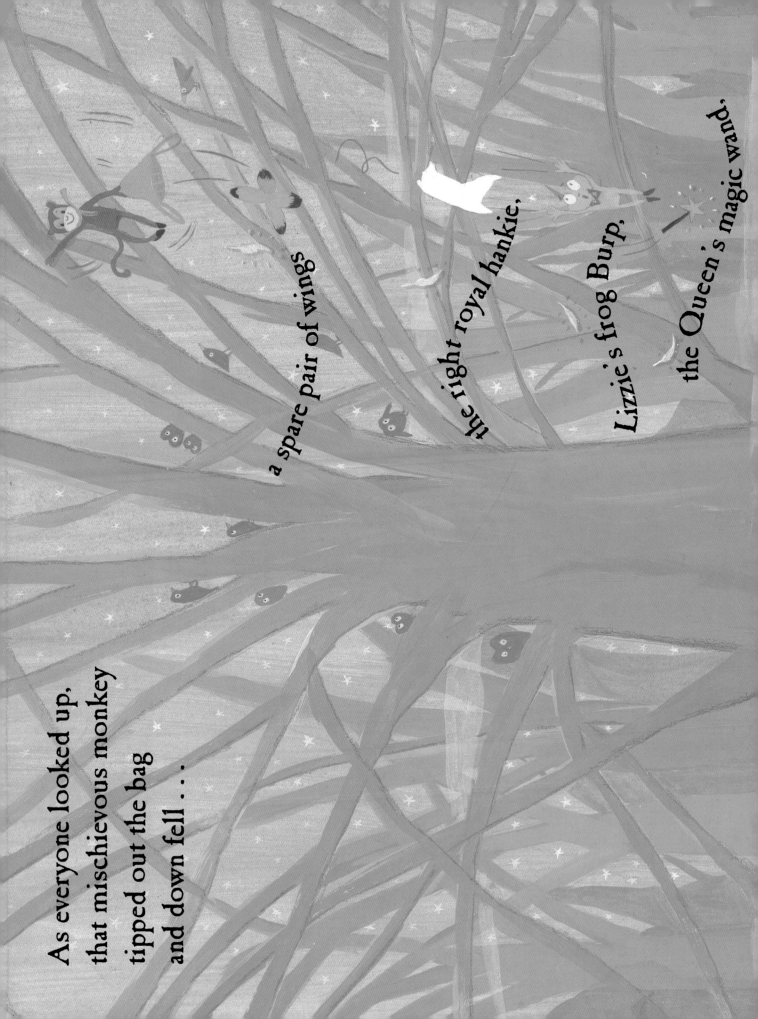

a spare pair of wings

the right royal hankie,

Lizzie's frog Burp.

the Queen's magic wand.

As everyone looked up,
that mischievous monkey
tipped out the bag
and down fell . . . .

and all the wishing feathers
the Queen had brought along for later.

The wand's magic was let loose.

Ellie's elephant started dancing.

Fiona's fox began to fly.

They caused such havoc,
it made the shark cry.

Feathers sprouted on Rabbit. Ears grew on the goose.
Gloria and Ben now had a gabbit and a roose!

Henry's hen laid a pen.

Betsy's bear looked like a pear.

And Bertie's bat became Bertie
and Bertie became his bat.

How crazy is that?

said Kirsty's cat.

And just as midnight struck, Burp handed the Queen her lost wand, and Lizzie gave back all the things from her bag.

With a wave of the wand,
all the madness and muddling stopped.
"I declare it's midnight!"
said the Queen.
"Let the feast begin."

And everyone sat down to a

FAIRY FEAST.

Fizzy Fudgecake

Star Pie

Chocolate Chips

Banana Pizza

Splodgy Pudding

Knickerbocker Glory

Carrot!

When everyone had eaten and it was time to go home,
the Queen gave them all a wishing feather.

She told them to close their eyes

and make a wish . . .

... and everyone's wish came true!

Even Burp's!

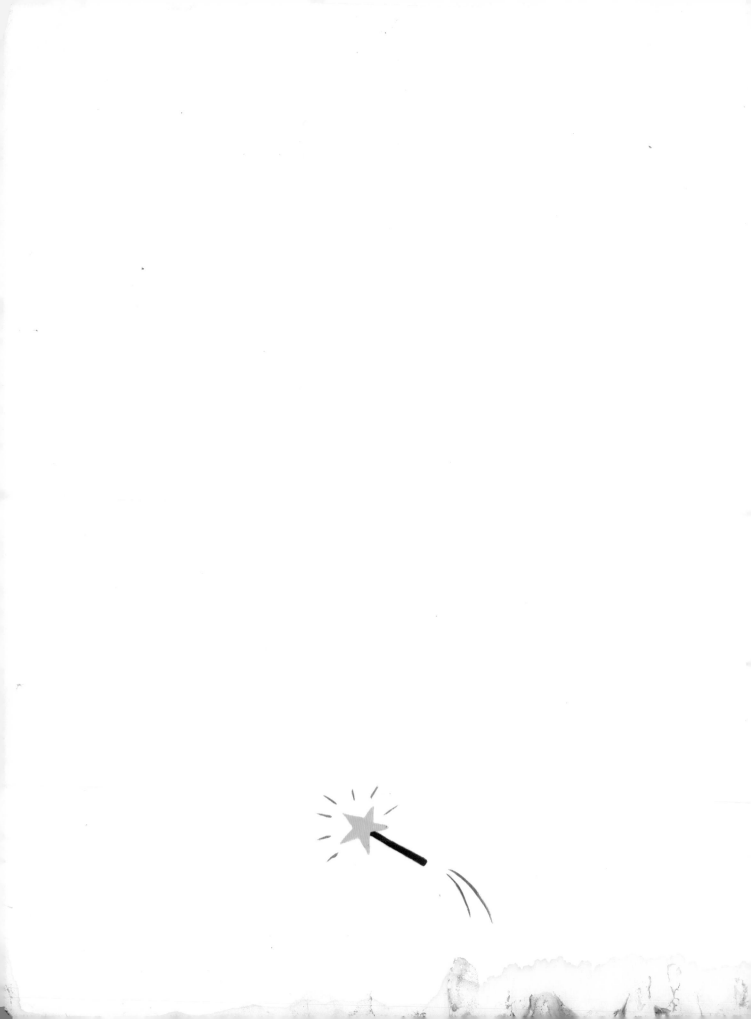